Y0-FBH-023

Futures

Also by Sandra Hochman

POEMS:

Voyage Home

Manhattan Pastures

The Vaudeville Marriage

Love Letters from Asia

Earthworks

NOVEL:

Walking Papers

FOR CHILDREN:

The Magic Convention

FILM:

Year of the Woman

DISCARD

FUTURES

New Poems by

SANDRA HOCHMAN

The Viking Press New York

Copyright © 1972, 1973, 1974 by Sandra Hochman
All rights reserved
First published in 1974 by The Viking Press, Inc.
625 Madison Avenue, New York, N.Y. 10022
Published simultaneously in Canada by
The Macmillan Company of Canada Limited
SBN 670-33323-9
Library of Congress catalog card number: 73-17785
Printed in U.S.A.
"Tap" originally appeared in *Antaeus*, "Angels Cook Dinner" in *Harper's Bazaar*, and "The Lover Goes Out like a Tooth" in *Ms.*

Acknowledgment is made to Grossman Publishers, Jonathan Cape Ltd., and the Estate of Pablo Neruda for the excerpt from *Twenty Love Poems and a Song of Despair* by Pablo Neruda, translated by W. S. Merwin. English language translation
Copyright © 1969 by W. S. Merwin. Reprinted by permission.

For Richard Grossman

Contents

Love is so short, forgetting is so long.

—PABLO NERUDA

Futures

Weary Love Poems

For Marc and Susan

1

The attraction: the pull
Of rope—tying me to dark eyes, eyes
Of lumber, and the mouth
Is ripe. How do I praise
The maker? In a building
Made of glass—under the neon
And the ordinary ceiling
A dark man is thinking, feeling—
Caught—in the rapture of what?
The agent of all things is this:
The desire to make love. To take
Legs, and arms, and arteries
And blood—and more than that blood
Flowing: a sigh—the breath—
And make it all
The film defeating death.

2

Or are you? Are you defeating
Death or merely flesh? Flesh the mother
And father—flesh the energy
And flesh the undresser. I remember
The immaculate King of Thule
Who ran away from his women and his tower
To set sail—one night—alone into
The sea. Weary of power. Not
You: you drink
The image in and feel the rope
Of everything that is possible. Unknown
People in unknown dreams—unknown
Movies of unknown images—unsaid
Words on unknown film: cuts that

Go from film to the skin. The film is this:
A way of extending yourself into everyone,
To sit back, for example, in a bathtub
And have your film in Barcelona, Peru, Santo Domingo,
Freeport, Normandy, to flash the image: SLEEP.

3

I see you. I sense you. Not as the
Maker despised by those out of power—
Not as the hero of a thousand "meetings"
Where telephones are powerful as death,
But as the dreamer, the small boy
Inside that never got enough—
Of touch, of kisses, of thighs, of
Wonder, of paper bags, of food, of things
That move and take you far away: airplanes
Swifter than the stream of blood,
Cars and the dark glasses of wine. Every day
A deal is made. Every day someone drops down
And the film industry flashes its own
Message: Awake awake. The industry—
That mistress with big tits larger than a goddess
And good enough to suck: the film world
Where business and teeth and power and lips
And aromas and sights take flight with the insane: the industry.

4

Some people are created to make
Mole hills. Or glaciers. You are
Not a mountain-climber—but a man
Who films the mountain. Can
Power be merely the flesh
That arms us for the battle: life or death?

Those who malign you
Secretly wish your wisdom: you, the
Quiet one—blessed
With your anger and pain. You want nothing
And encompass everything. Nothing holds you
Longer than perfection: you seek it
In deals, columns of numbers, film, images—
And you want nothing except All. You want the All.
All that you make is All. That is why
I trust you, find in your eyes
A word
For everything: see in your eyes
A known quantity: Energy.
And more than that—deep feeling—
The feeling one has when one
Wants nothing. How to explain it?
The detached man: satisfied
With nothing—driven
Like a wild animal
To forget the lazy world of
Clocks and possibilities—the armed
Hero out to create—
A film. Come back
With colors, words, faces, the excitement
Of a city—come home with pelts
Of flesh and power—and it is for this
That I lay under your arm
Breathing your smell into me. It was the smell
Of lumber, smell of hemp, smell of film
When it flaps against the
Odd machine that splices
And then splices again. No one

Wants more than you. No one seeks
Less power. You—who have
Covered yourself in numbers and have
Not taken your name across the screens of Europe, South America, Asia
For nothing. I see you. I see
The strong boy. The proud person
That never got out.

Walking the Walls

As I am following my
Toes up the wall, I know that another place exists,
Somewhere else, where women, for example,
Are not climbing the walls. In another
Place palm trees bend in the sun—the green
Joints of the great sensual palms open their
Fronds, paradise in the palms, opening
Like hands. People I do not remember
Wait to welcome me. They identify me
As the woman who always carries a picture
Of her daughter next to her hat or her
Heart. I am often found
Waiting to go back
To the Center of the Earth, the hollow earth,
I know it is there, by all that is true,
I know it is there—beyond snow—
A place where children play, where people
Are not afraid of affection, where there
Is order and no fear of time. The Center of
The Earth is there for those who know
That kindness is everything, and love
Doesn't have to be scarce as uranium. Anyway,
I'm up on the walls today
Like an upside-down tiger, looking at walls,
Staring at them under my feet,
As always, writing pictures that resemble
Screams, as always writing a documentary
On loneliness, shooting it all in my head—
The whole asylum that is here in your papers—
Shooting it all in my head—the documentary
Writing—on the walls.

I Have

I have an aunt who hates marriage and sells wedding
Dresses to brides, sometimes to men
After the store is closed—those brides who cannot
Be seen during day hours, my favorite aunt—

I have an uncle who I always knew was the best man
There is, an uncle selling Campco trucks in Florida,

I have an uncle who lives in California and packages
Dirty soap which he sends all over the world, who
Lives like a hermit lives in his shed of leaves,

I have an ex-boyfriend who walks through the streets
Of Manhattan in tweeds and has grown his hair so long
He resembles a sage, a man who is lonely and does
Not belong on television—that is where he is seen—
A person once removed from any real dimension—

I have an ex-husband who carries around his clippings
In a pocketbook from Greece, a man who loves to identify
Himself to himself,

I have a friend called Jane who comes with me and
My daughter and my daughter's friends to the park where
We go down the slides and I laugh as I go down the
Slide and say "This is my office" as I'm sliding down
To the bottom then climb up again—

I have a friend called Judith who worked with me on
Secret film projects—

I have a lot of pain—

I have a child who blows balloons and is learning how
To punch,

I have a lot of debts—
I have an ex-agent, ex-hubs of wheels that were once
Marriage, I have poems in my brain float in
Water all day long, floating like leaves in water—

I have a need to see women ennobled and to become what
History has never allowed them to be—equal to others—

I have a friend called Ti-Grace who walks down the
Street wearing glasses that sit on her eyes like two
White saucers and a halo that sits on her red
Kerchief and that is her radiance as she walks down
Seventy-ninth Street carrying a brown paper-bag—

I have a friend called Flo who is all sunlight and
Truth and nothing will ever erase her heart from that
Board where true hearts are drawn in gold chalk—

I have a new family doctor who gave me a questionnaire
Asking about my mucus, my eyes, my limbs, my stool, my
Lungs, my colds, and I said yes to everything—

I have a new family in a group of elevator men who
Work in my building and they have seen me crying a
Lot as I go up and down in the elevator—

I have a favorite palm tree world in
The country of Ceylon where I want to go—

I have a great interest in the myth of America—the
Myth America who worked for nothing and was always
A volunteer—

I have a friend whom I admire called Betty Harris whom
I want to write a book with called "A Couple of Bucks"
Or Bucks—a book about women's need to be
Independent—
I have a world that is in the center of the
Earth that I go to—
I have a dog that rarely goes to the moon, who
Never jumps over the moon,
I have a friend whom I love who lives in my house
And it is because of these
Things—because of the old newspapers which wrap
Up my old life as if it were an old fish with the
Scales smelling—
I have a heart that is never tired of loving,
I have a pair of white shoes that I put on every
Morning,
I have a friend in Brazil who makes palm trees out
Of feathers, who farms and creates with earth instead
Of colors,
I have friends in Chile, my best friends in Chile—
I
Have
I have I have

As a Young Healthy Girl

I danced at the Copacabana. I see myself
As a young girl dancing on the arm
Of my father. I hear the rolling drums
Under the hands of the bored drummer. I hear
Forks and knives scraping against the plates,
Hear the sounds the Mafia-men and the garbage-men
Make as they bang their spoons, hear the jokes
Come over the microphone. I am
Going upstairs to a strange room to see
Frankie Laine. I am "introduced" to him
By a friend of my father. I am given a glossy
Face shot of Frankie Laine. He signs it saying
"Thank you." I take the photo back to
Boarding school. I wonder "Thanks for what?"
He sings "Mule Train" using his whip in my
Head. I am shy. I am frightened of everything
Even mules. I am dancing on the arm of my
Father. At the Stork Club. At the blue starry
Copacabana. In my wandering years, wondering
What was the matter. Something inside me was wrong.
I had no idea that my strangeness, my
Wilderness lonely, my not being anyone at all, my
Fear I did not exist, no one would keep
Me for long—was only
Balanced by dreaming, writing, green thoughts,
Flower cluster white over green, my own song,
My own journey into a deeper self; but for the
Moment
I dance at the Copacabana—something is wrong—
I look too much like my father.

Palm Song

I have spent a lot of my time
Doing ordinary things. I have known
Loss more than my own face in the mirror.
I have given a drawing to everyone I adore.
I pay attention to life that is interior.
I seek perfection. See it in crayons.
I have been pasted against paper.
Some days a beloved woman comes walking
With me. Saint Joan. Saint Theresa. Or
Flo Kennedy. Sometimes I go out walking
With divine words inked in my soul
Like so many flowers that enfold and fold.
I walk with glacier lilies, with the iris
And daisy, with straw flowers.

I have spent a lot of my time
Doing ordinary things. And I have lived in
Tropical places. I have lived with jade vine,
Lobster claw, Canna, African tulip and Allamanda.
I have been in exile. I have sought perfection.
And I have found that touching
Gives both heat and light.

I Have Known a Lot of Women

With peritonitis,
Women who smoked and drank
In the Bougainvillea, women who wanted
To be genius-free and mopped their lives
Like dust into a pan that emptied
Where? Where did it go?

I have loved
Myself as a woman even
Though I am filled, often,
With rage, love to find
The height where I can jump
Even higher. If you ask me "What
Is your essence?" I would not tell
You Fern, Oats, Barley, Carrot,
Spring Onion, Cabbage, whatever is
Divine, wondrous, strange. I look
In my blood-stream for a future
Adequate to my needs. I look in my body
For an answer.
                    Arms I love your arms.
Feet I love your feet. Fronds of blood fan
Out. The nose is all. I sniff
                                    myself.

Acting It Out

On the brink of becoming a female
Comedienne, leaving for Boston to try my act out
At the Racquet Club of Hyannis with the
Supremes, I stop and think of the past. Night-
Mares of you continue to haunt me
Like dirty jokes you cannot forget. The old
Life slips off quietly like an act
You try to get out of. It's lonely standing
Up here, saying what you know is true,
And not sure that anyone gets you.

Radiant Armor

For Pat

I looked for a knight in shining armor. One day
I woke up and became that knight myself.
It happens: You begin wearing a pair of
Glowing socks, old rubber-soled shoes that make you
Light as helium. It starts then in reality, shoes
And socks. The rest is simple. It is what
You think that you become. As you once mentioned
While you were sitting in front of the steam-beck
And tangling and untangling the bright film
As one untangles water—thoughts are things. You
Are wearing it: the vest of crab and gray pelican,
Gull and heron's breast, shining,
Feather, whistling scales that let us float
Also in your universe: all joy. The way the
Film is. Your armor.

Do not take it off. Do not waken in
Your old pajamas, wear the thing, the light
Around the small hairs of your arms, the
Silver galaxy that goes on the body. I have worn
It too, in the dark night, when the city slept and
I was sleeping. I went out in dreams. No one heard
Me. I was not suspected.

Armor is a natural material. It is not
Different from velvet, silk, or wash-and-wear
Nylon. Now nothing can hurt you. Nothing
Can ever hurt you.

But sometimes you have to snail-dance
From the claws of love. From love—the lobster—
With its shell filled with green. All the
World loves a lover—and yet—when you consider
The arguments, arrangements, the lack of
Touch and taste—all the world loves a lobster—
Said the woman, strangling in green roe—
We survive the crunch.

Once
A long team ago, a long term ago, time
In time out ago, I was married to a guy
Called Franco. "Franco, do you mind
If I go in a corner of the room and write?" I would
Ask, practically sucking on my thumb. Franco,
A fuddler, a fiddler-arounder, a violinist, would
Keep me, a prisoner of sound, in the studio,
While I listened to him practice. "Please, Franco,
Can't I write a little bit?" "You can
Always write later on," he would say. His fingers
Were insured.

You can't imagine
What it's like
To make love
With a guy
Whose fingers are insured by Lloyd's
Of London. Like it or not you
Can't demand that he touch you "There"
Or "There" or "Here" or even touch
You at all with those insured fingers. Suppose
Over your breast a finger broke, or a knuckle

Went out of whack? If a finger goes
Wrong the whole hand goes—life-line and all.

You might as well crawl
Back in your shell. All the world
Loves a lobster.

Futures

For Renée Schwartz

For several moments or several months or several years
I have been raising money. Fundraising is timeless—makes
You think, sometimes, that past and future are contained
In gold bricks, melted down, to the yield of the sun. Or green,
Backs—bucks—are the real thing you are after.

"There's poetry in fundraising," I said to myself. And
Someone said over the phone, "In the capitalist system
The only spiritual cure is money." I am out to cure myself. That

Is a fact. Of what? I am not sure. It is true
That I have heard visions, that is, I hear
People speaking to me on a regular basis. What do they speak
About? These people talk about

Exaggerations. My life down to the last
Corpuscle has been a nightmare of exaggerations. My baby's nurse
Doesn't come home. She comes home mugged. Her purse has
Been stolen. I go away on a vacation
And my clothes are taken. I raise money
For a movie that is exaggerated visions on a screen. I dream
In weird deposits of images on screens. Movies, I tell myself,

Are the fiberglass shadows of those people.

Producers. All possible investors. One was an ex-football
Captain, another the leader of the New Jersey nightclub Mafia
Who promised me he's going to see
About loose money lying around. Lying around
In the spaghetti bags, or gardens, like weeds. Am
I a poet bound to be backed by the mob? What could I say
To the Mafia market? The women's market I know
About: respect, self-confidence go over big

With the new group of recently discharged from the insane
Asylum called marriage. The F.B.I. of the solar
System is now tracking down the women's markets.

Even before I went into fundraising
Everything had changed, I knew that people dealt in
Poems, futures, —"We want to tie you up,"
Said the guy sitting across from me yesterday at exactly this
Time, although it seems years ago. "Of course if it turns out
You have any talent we want an exclusive—a first
Right of refusal if you know what we mean—why should we back you
Unless you come back to us?" Tie me up? I want to shout

But do not dare. Tie up my nose? Tie up my lips?
My underarm odor? My shoes, my dreams, my stomach pains? My vulva
And aorta? My mucus? My depressions? My snowy dreams of
Childhood when it rained and rained and rained and nothing ever
Happened to me sexually and that was the time when Gussie Schwartz
With red hair and tiny red arm-hairs decided that I would be his
Girlfriend when we kissed? What does a personal life mean

To me now? It is not as good as fundraising. Nay. It interferes
With fundraising. With my future. Although I see future
Coming toward me in the form of yield and pari-passu profit
With one for you and one for me. I cannot recall how I got into

Profits and losses. I am certain
That I am a secret multimillionaire of the saga of
Angels. General partner. Investor in
The fate of everyone. Breakneck
Boss of the green buck, mommy bucks, climbing the
Heralaya in herstory, queen of the conglomerate
Mogul world where everything—everything—is

Worth fighting for. Time is
Money, time is exaggerated, time
Is nothing real except that what was once funny is
Now becoming ridiculous.

And I am on call back and yield my tongue and
Eyes to whoever wants tongue and eyes.

Girlhood Was Being Curious

For Jerry Goldsmith

The more
I live, the more
I die. Should I
Take off for Florida and
Fish, demonstrate
On streetcorners the snowed-up
Guts of the broken world? The more

I love, the more I die, oh, don't forget
Me Vergara Grez, painter of sunsets in Chile,
And you, the copper woman of the copper fields,
Or you, sweet peasant woman who said
"It is better to give than to have." I the
Jubilation of giving
Away myself
To anyone. Girlhood was being
Curious, jubilant, curious,
Girlhood was discovering again and again
The difficulty of being first,
The heartache of wanting to be more
Than left behind, than waiting: girlhood was
Wanting to have, then wanting to give.

Running for Office

I put on my tap shoes and on an old truck
Parked in the middle of Central Park
I tapped my heart out
    one two
    one two
For Shirley Chisholm. Have you any idea
What it means to be president?

To be president you need
The soft-holy-shoe of a poet.

Talking to Women

I would like to write the biographies
Of Matilda, Ti-Grace, Flo, Diane—Renée and
Alexandra—all of them—

On the empty white paper. Matilda, courageous
Fighter of the absurd against the normal. Ti-Grace,
Honest in your bones, dancing in your bones.
Flo—"When I was little
My papa told me I was somethin', my mama
Told me I was somethin', by the time I found
Out I was nothin'—it was too late—I already
Felt like somethin' "—

I wrote some
Postcards, after my dictionary divorce
I looked myself up under S (surrealist) and did
Not find myself, then looked myself up under
H (hag) and nothing doing, I looked myself
Up under Courage, under Comedian, under Delegate,
Under Mother, under Bombshell—and I'm still
Looking.

My Nurse

Nursie. My first memory—secrets
Crying aloud—of a birthday, was putting
My backside in the air like a cake of pink
Flesh and having myself spanked for good luck
By my nurse—one—two—three—years were
Spankings in the roly-poly days of cues
And tears and cribs. Am I really supposed to
Remember all this?

I live there still. In the world of
White hands, white knuckles, blocks, decals,
Stars for good things, clothes picked up, no
Tears. I live there. In the round galaxy of
The roly-poly doll, the prison of the crib,
The Catholic cross. The first great separation
Was her loss.

We were friends. More than lovers, more than
Child and mother, we were two spies in the house
Of my parents. She was Nursie—Helen Cohan. I
Was barefoot tough-girl Sandy. Strangers in
The argument world of Sid and Mae where neither
Of us belonged. I threw footballs at her pillows.
We were two spies—we stuck together
In our room of plants and turtles, books,
Dolls, shiny shoebags for my shoes—her
Large shoes I wore to try the future on with
My toes. Nurse—Nurse—

Hitler
And bare rooms, divorce and parents
Living upside down, mother selling
Bathrobes, living with grandparents,

You in a brownstone, Daddy in a tiny
Black hotel and you, arriving during
A boarding-school vacation, to take me
To the movies and my screaming (I had
Not seen you in two years) *Mommy Nurse*
Has A Hunch On Her Back and Mother:
You didn't know that?

The past: Large vines of blue across the
Knuckles of my nurse, kind hands, holding
My flesh, washing me, comforting me, large
Veins, white gnarled hands. Nursie,
When we were in the green fields
Governing
Robin's eggs with the heels of our hands
And cupping them, fragile, from the nest
To our skin, Nursie, I loved you, great
Dark-haired friend, my first love, first world,
Who hugged me to her breast in the black night
When I feared everything, Nursie, who taught
Me to pray, to love Nature, to love
All living things except myself—Nurse nurse
I climb that ghostly tree
Where you hold up your long white arms to
Catch me
And from the past my limbs, my veins, my guts
And hair my kidneys lungs nostrils nightmares
Come falling down
Where you try to hold me up, try to catch me.
But I fall down
And am still falling down.

Women

Women are often found
Dead at the top of their poems but
I am doing something else this winter. I'm
Fishing in Florida not for fish mind you
But for something else. An old
China-hand I'm fishing for a way to live
My life. I pull a poem—babble—out
Of water hold it in my hand—

Poets are often found breathing but
Their gills remain lifeless and they go back
To water, off the hook, thrown back too small
To take for dinner or be stuffed
To hang as trophies on a mantelpiece. Women
Are often found dead, poets found, women found.

Women are often found dead at the tops of
Their lovers.

Tap

Shuffle. Flap. I have dreamt of hoofers
In Paradise—the legs two small machines
Spreading wings, perfect as airplanes—
                                        Shuffle
And the sand spread on the tap board
Of Sandman Sims—his own world of
Rhythm—think of the top of a drum
With the sound the drumsticks make—
                                        Tap
Or think of being numb in hell
Then suddenly being freed by your own
Sounds.
                        Toe. Heel. Flap. Shuffle. Flap.
Inside the mirror of the dance studio with Jerry Ames
On Seventy-second Street I see a reflection
Of the dancer. I have taken myself seriously. Now
There is nothing left of me but this: a time
Step. A lesson in suffering myself. An hour with
The master going "Shuffle. Toe. Hell
Is surmounted by my toes." I almost forget
My pain. I cry out "It is very plain
That I am born to tap. I am a natural dancer."

I look in the mirror of my toe, a shiny silver tap
That may undo
Hell and Heaven and the raw life too! Flap. Heel. Toe.
Shuffle. Flap. Heel. Tap.

The Lover Goes out Like a Tooth

Yippee. I am without you. Yanked
The old tooth out. You were a moldy hairy
Tooth, cancerous in my throat. You
Pained me. Nothing helped. Not aspirin.
Not vitamin. Not the mineral
Of sperm (a mute dear thing inside me).
You are out of my mouth. I am toothless.
Cannot talk. How funny to look at my gums
And nothing there. No teeth.
                                        Red root,
                                        No wisdom tooth.
Feeling gone. I'm a mute. No toothache.
No pain. But I cannot chew. And will
Not love you. Tooth tooth
At night I remember you. Oh, Oh—the pain
How sharp, how good, how wondrous
My strength. You inside me, cooing on my gums,
Giving me power to chew, to masticate, bit
The weird thistle, root
Now. Nothing to eat. Cannot chew. Cannot
Speak. Empty round mouth
With no pain. Only a hole.
A hole which I cover
With the mask of my swollen lip. Nothing
Is no teeth. No one in my mouth. No old tooth
That kept me
Aware aware aware.

Love Poems

THE MEMORY 1

How to place back memory, push it back out of the head
When it comes rolling out of the cavities of the brain like
Too much foam? I lie in bed, a hard-hat, pushing my shoulders
Against the memory. Pushing it back. I lie there. Hard facts
Grow large as foam molds. I am growing old. Blonde. Thirty-seven.
I remember when the odd was even.

What it meant to be married was this: My
Name was Mrs. We lived together. From the
Very beginning something was the matter. Ivry locked
Me up in a cabinet in Paris. An apartment where I played
Rapunzel. But no prince came. I sat there, trying to
Learn French, sitting in the bathroom when he played
The violin. This is what was happening: two people trying
To avoid each other. He played in the afternoons. I sat
And listened. Tried not to make too much noise. I was an
Appendage to the guy. He needed me like a hole in the
Head. I severed my connections with the living—my parents,
All my friends—teachers and talented odds and ends—and
Stayed around him waiting for a life. He was my life-guard
And the buoys. He was the ocean and make no mistake—
It's all in the past: but remember. I learned to live without him,
BUT SECRETLY I REMAINED HIS WIFE.
I became a liar in Paris as his wife. It wasn't easy and
It became my life. (It started like this: one affair with
A married man, and sneaking about kept me quiet.)
Excuses must be made when you go out for bread and come
Back with marmalade. I began changing. Went shopping more
Often: secretly, in the crummy back hotels
Of Paris, which all were brothels.
He loved me. Made me whole—affairs
Are for the liars of the world.

MEMORY 2

I remember looking
For apartments in Paris. Up stairs
And down stairs. I remember looking for apartments
In Paris: leaks and cold water. A phone call from
My father: "My daughter
Shouldn't be running around
With a bunch of no-good artists." Instead
I rented a car without a hood
And drove somewhere in the country—
Normandy—to
Be myself whoever she was. I grew and grew. Suddenly
I woke up breathing through gills. I had turned
Into a sea-maiden and set out for the dangerous place
Under the water. There I saw my father:
"You have come home" he said
To me. I stood there drowning.

PARIS 3

Elegant women
Are carrying their groceries in
A bag of string. Under the crown of
A hat a madman goes
About his business, cheerful
And unwilling to admit
That his therapy is the
Careful display of hair. Flamelike
Ripplings
Over the fountain—and there—
Something horrible—myself as
I used to be when I lived in Paris—
Undisciplined, unruly, wearing
Velvet slacks worn out and filled with urine

In the crotch, old sweater,
Hair over my eyes, looking
Mournfully at studios, windows,
Cathedrals, fruit
Stalls, walking for four years
On familiar streets, saying depressing
Things, revolted by ornaments—
A fake as it turned out. I always carried
Within me this bee's sack of joy.

Babar

Is sitting at home in his easy chair. Babar
Decides it is less tiring to watch himself on television
And so he sits in front of TV. He sees himself
In a play. A comedy. I ram my way through the audience
And say to Babar "Speak to me
And say something nice to me." Babar is speaking to me
Again. He always used to speak to me. When
I was a child he comforted me. He always had
Good things to do in that book where he lived
With all the writing. He made me happy. Babar
I have looked for you in all the weirdest places
But have not found you. Babar—you are without a doubt
From that noble race of elephants—the history
Of the elephant is fraught with tragedy.
From the top of my heart
To the bottom of my ankles: I have grown up lonely.

Amagansett

For Harout

We stand up in each other's arms
Secretly taking root. You turn my arms

Into a bed. I hold your face
In my fingers. "I've died"

I said "And now I've gone to heaven."

I Want to Tell You

In Memory of Pablo Neruda

I want to tell you what it feels like not to touch.
It's terrible. Your head blows up
Until it feels like a balloon floating somewhere
And your feet are filled with helium and your light
In the sky—only nothing is there. No arm, no wrist,
No thigh. The thighs go first. Feeling gone.
Then the nipples. Then your arms.

Not to make love is unbearable.
Taking hold of the resting place you
Bob into sleep, but it isn't sleep. It isn't relief—it's
The sleep of the prisoner with the terrible bars
Of the body shining in the distance. And that's why the womb
Shines like linoleum
Under the stars, marvelous in its pursuit
Of a poor piece of flesh that will lovingly
Cover it up. Oh hear me, amazons, mistresses, wives,
Let air fly through the body, let all women dance
Into kingdoms of where loving is not getting even.

Bleeding

For Al Imhoff and Jacqueline Swartz

In bed my life has started bleeding again.
Out of my pores, out of the strange sun-pores of blood
Come mother and father warning me not to be a
Wise-guy. Out of my pores come all the teachers who
Made me hate reading and writing—and suddenly out of
My body come the merciless men who took my
Eyes and lips and body—my first husband playing the violin
Spills out of my skin—I no longer can rest with him
Putting my face under the security of his blond hair
Which came out of his arm—there
Are the other monsters there—the poet who turned out
To be berserk, the comedian-jerk, the pilot who lied,
The strange blue-eyed Italian boy who drove with me through
Scotland, and the husband who could not like me. I am
Bleeding now too much. Take a mop.
All this blood shall be clotting on the bed. There is
No one here
Giving my signs away, my secrets stay with me, but
The albumen comes out, with legs of dead loves
That begin to clot.

Children's Court

1

I remember the children's court. At first
I thought it would be a court of silk dresses
And jesters with jingle bells on the ends of felt
Wands, place of silk and gauze and princesses. Fat,
Blonde, nervous, anxious about whether or not I got
To live with my mother or father or no one at all
(Would I be left dying of touch-hunger in the hall?)
I waited, oh, I waited for the day. The court
Was a large empty room with folding chairs. I went
In the bathroom to puke with my Aunt Anne holding my head
Saying "Choose your mother if the judge asks who you love
Best." My father didn't pass the test. He sat
Wearing his old gray felt hat, half-blind, with no one
Beside him. He was weeping openly. Why had this
Happened to him? Why was he being humiliated in a large
Room not able to touch his child who sat across from him
And waved with her seven-year-old hand—across the
Court where he was all alone?

2

There is no lesson learned by the child from divorce. I
Wondered why my mom and dad hated each other. Now I know
Hostility is easier than love. Expectations, fantasies
Are built into the foundations of our years, pumped into
Our arteries: so much to have, so much to want. We want
What we are not.

3

I imagine my mother and father as they must have been
Before the great disaster: me. He was a millionaire by the
Time he was sixteen—working his guts out on the streets of
The city—paper-vending at five, carrying suitcases for nickles,

At seven running errands on the street, skipping school. There
Wasn't much to eat in my father's house on Saint Mark's Street. My
Grandmother—who looked like a combo between Eleanor Roosevelt
And Danny Kaye—was always looking the other way. My father's brothers
Died of poverty at the age of twelve. My grandfather—who sold
Orangeade at Coney Island (my father called him a minstrel—
When he could—my dad—exaggerated
It was all he had—) singing PURE SUGAR NO BLUFFS
To the suckers on the boardwalk. Handsome. Spendthrift. My grandfather
Went from the pushcart to the coffin. Dying in a poor-house, epileptic
And near mad—he called for my dad. "Save me, take me out of here,
Me my son." My father—helpless, could not take his father
From that prison. And imprisoned us—in anger, brutality, cheapness, miserliness,
And lies. He—my father—victim of the cage
Where his own father died, was filled with rage.
My grandmother—his mother—carried on. She was a janitor
And mopped the shit and piss of all the unglamorous. She saved (green) loaves
Her money in the stove. One day it burned. She mopped and saved again, again
Until her sons—three that were left—made "men" out of themselves. Her sons
Were men.

4

For my Uncle Joe, my father's brother, I can speak
Without tears because I loved him best. His name in pool-rooms on the lower
East Side was STRETCH—probably because he was so tall
He didn't stretch at all. The legends say my
Uncle Joe—who never went to school—was a gay
Blade, a ladies' man. Tall, deep-voiced, with a moustache,
Twisted fingers with the nails ripped off in various
Accidents, amazing energy, he married a woman known
As Tess in the family mess. While married to Tess
He met Marie and while divorcing Tess in Vegas for Marie
He married someone else. Married to all three

Put him in jail for bigamy. Or trigamy. He shmeared his
Way out of things and wound up with Marie—
A great lady—and made his fortune in lumber it was said—
Calling his company INTEGRITY flooring although he didn't
Know what the word meant and took it from an advertisement
On the radio for Squibb toothpaste. He built a castle in
Philadelphia. To me—he was heavenly. I loved to visit the
Uncle Joe–Aunt Marie castle. She always had big
Aquamarine rings which looked like ice cubes on her fingers. In
Her bedroom were bottles filled with the smells of
Jasmine and roses. Her clothes which I inspected as a brat—
Opening her closets—were all lace and velvet and so soft.
I loved her hands. Her large white breasts. Her lips
And Uncle Joe's papaness. I was afraid of him too—seeing him lose
His temper and go into a rage. He threatened to kill my
Mother if he saw her. I feared for my mother. Uncle Joe, it was said,
Had killed a man, had been in jail. It wasn't true. Gentle soul, I
Loved him for his wit, his audacity, his rage. He was
Not afraid to exaggerate. Only his voice betrayed his
Courage. Uncle Joe gave me (can I forget?)
My first gold bracelet. It had a heart on it. I lost it in the Roxy.
It was the first great loss
Of precious things. And then I lost my house.

5

My father's tears. My father's tears. Can I forget my father's
Tears? A great fat blubber of a man who lost his wife.

Addict

In bed I lie still, sweating my life out.
It is with you, the addicts (the mad ones)
That I am comfortable. You are the aristocrats
That I underestimated: I spied on your
Misery until I became one of you.
I know you: odd sister of the alphabet—addicted to the final
Act of childhood—the writing of poems
Poems of starscapes. And you—addict of love—
My dream sister—the dreamer in my flesh—the oddball in me
That tried to break away and couldn't. Kill the old self.
DEATH & REBIRTH
Is a passion of sorts. Like alcohol, junk, politics
It's a dirty sport. At night, brothers and sisters
Of the weakness and no will—at night—me the spy reporter—
I jump out of the window sill and hang holding on to the hand
Of my other—my shadow in my sleep. O mother
Me said the girl holding on. "Fall" said the addict, closer
To death and life than all the others. All of the
Them turn into heroines: I lie still—carelessly killing myself
In my bed, sweating and dreaming. Papa & Mama who will not love
Me, to whom I am addicted, lie close to me
Breathing and lying in their own dreams of leaving. I am in
Quest of a miracle: in quest of death and
Rebirth. In my dream I drop from the hand holding me and fall down
The twenty stories of the building, fall past all the windows—
And—being something of a spy comedian—
Cannot resist this last chance to snoop on other people's lives.
DROPPING
DEAD CAN BE FUN I think, turning in the air, dropping, sensuously
Like a pebble from the top floor, in the glassy window sills I see
Men and women cooking each other in a marital stew, see
Children blowing bubbles, see immovable blackness coming from TV
And in the faces of my neighbors I see no defeat—no kindness—
Only shock—to see me falling from the rooftop.

Secrets of Wonder Women

For my daughter Ariel and her friend Laura Strausberg

Let them
Eat cake said
Marie Antoinette. I would be satisfied with bread. Or pancakes.
Or anything tasty. I sadly look into the empty world of no rice, no
potatoes. It's sad to live in a world without noodles.

I am now in the no-noodle world. No-cake world. It's lonely here. I
go out to dinner and see people actually eating bread. It becomes
less like a discipline, more like a torture. I want to rush up to
the thin woman in the restaurant and say: Do you know how lucky you
are? Do you know what it means to be allowed to have butter in your
life? What if I have talent, a child, a home, a
daddy-replacement, seven secret lovers, and I'm making my own movie? It
all means nothing if I can't eat butter. Or noodles. Or cake.

Food. I love you, food.

I am now on a diet.

The diet clinic is in the middle of the city. I am given my food in
little tin trays. It is called the Kennedy Clinic. Thomas Mann might
have written about it. It is almost a sanatorium. It is so neat and
clean and there are always nice sounds coming out of the radio. The
white bag is filled with diet food. I felt better the first week.

Now I feel awful. I have been trying to cope with weight for so
long I can't stand it. Waves of hunger come over me. I have
cut everything good to eat out of my life. It's a shame to live
this way.
And
I have to. In order to stay thinner than I was. I used to be a large
balloon. Now I'm a small balloon. Pop.

About flattery: my life as a young goddess was spent in girdles.
Other goddesses wore pants. They were ladies. Eleven years old: I remember
girdles. Thick girdles to pull in my stomach. I suffered in rubber girdles.
The kindest thing about a rubber girdle which made your seat feel like
a rubber tire was that when you took it off you felt suddenly that
you had changed from a reptile into a human. The rubber skin which
I wore to hold in my tummy. At sixteen I wanted to be well dressed and
gorgeous. The styles were all for thin goddesses. I was a chubby. The ads
in the mags were all for no-hip no-breast no-fanny goddesses. I wore old
sweaters and old shirts. My friends were all somber and thin. I grew up
fat and funny. And then when no one was looking and no one cared I
sailed away. One day I moved to Hong Kong. I made friends with a doctor
called Doctor Carey Hughes who was handsome and charming and looked like
Cary Grant. He said "Have you no discipline? I'm going to put you on
a diet. You have to come and see me every week for vitamin
injections. I want you to lose weight." I lost weight. Just for the
excuse to see him. I would have taken off a thousand pounds just to
be admitted to his presence. I went from one hundred and fifty to one hundred
and five pounds. I would have kept on dieting just to go to his office. I would
have gone down to thirty-three pounds if I could just go on seeing
Doctor Carey Hughes. But he was called away on business to America.
Suddenly I was one hundred pounds and in Hong Kong. Boy, did I get
busy with tailors. I had thousands of days wearing fat-goddesses' clothes
to make up for. I slinked around with my new figure. I bought sexy
underwear, it was wonderful. No breasts. No ass. No nothing. But thin.
It was the thinnest time of my life.

Why? Because in the flesh of my fantasy I remained wonder woman.
When I'm fat I'm nervous. I'm a fatty, a roly poly, a butterball.
My life has been a history of pounds. At the time I was born I
weighed seven pounds, I now weigh a hundred and twenty-seven.
The story of the hundred and twenty in between seven is the story

of my life. I can best describe myself as someone who would like to feel
weightless. To be thin, almost invisible. To hardly be there.

What does it mean to be weighed down by weight? Flesh, when there
is too much of it, takes the lightness out of life. The chip off
the old block is often too big a chip. But down to fleshy facts:
we eat to love ourselves. It is no accident that we eat our hearts
out but put on our hips. Some of the kindest most talented people
I have known have been fat. When you're fat the world transforms
itself—the fats are the outs the thins are the ins.

Many pounds ago I was a goddess in boarding school who paid great
attention to my body. I knew the secrets of the adrenal glands inside
out—I watched my ballooning body puff into huge mounds of flesh.

Confessions of a fat goddess: I always wanted to be thin. My fleshery
was a prison. I felt like a loaf of bread growing thicker and thicker
in the life oven.

Nobody loves a fat goddess. A fat goddess is usually someone who doesn't
listen to advice. And so to be a heroine, flying in the galaxy, it's
diet until death.

Finding the Center

I am a witch. A wicked woman. A trouble-maker.
Oh I STILL
Lament for my head. Lament for the dead. Dinner's on. No one comes.
I am a single mother. I have
A single daughter. We live in a single house.
Hot and cold water. We have a nurse who must
Go to the hospital for cataracts. We have bills
To be paid. And a lot of time in the house.
I am a single mother. I have no one
But myself
To warm me in bed
And rub me down. A man comes my way
And looks funny to me: his eyes have thistles
The way roses once did. I am a single mother.
I am alone forever. My breast has gone
Into the refrigerator. My ears are frozen
In the ice container. Whatever joy I had
Molds in a plastic bag. Once, and it was a long
Time ago, perhaps a thousand feathers ago,
I preened and tried to be young. I kept trying. Now
Death seems like an ice show. I am
Often caught in the middle of dreaming. What
Are you thinking of? I am thinking
Of the way it was when I was a child. Nowhere
To go. No place to hide.
                    I am a bitch. A trouble-maker. A good woman.

Angels Cook Dinner

For Lee Guber

1

Who are angels? Where do they come from?
They speak in voices that I understand. They live
In ghettos where they break into laments. They cook.
They are the heralds
Of ordinary things. They open
Doors with salt and cauliflowers and leaves of gentle spinach.

Holidays are a time
To seek angels. To look for them
And ask for what is missing in the heart of the lettuce.
Angels come out of the ocean like huge waves
Who salt the sand and tell us above the sound of water
What we are and what we must become.

2

Who are angels? They are children breaking open their hearts
And telling you about their lives. My daughter Ariel is an
Angel. She tells me about a restaurant where her uncle took her
For lunch called the Embers. Why is it called Embers? Because
It has a lot of Ems. "You can't swim" someone said to me in a
Rowboat. Ariel said "My mother can't swim but she can write. . . ." Angels are
Five-year-old people whose arms when they hold you are soft
Feathers that are the spring-source of fire. When I open a book that
I love I enter the life of an angel. Angels are you and you and
You—submerged strangers to whom I throw the alphabet, seamarks
Of my life.

3

I played an angel in the Christmas pageant at boarding school. I hated
Boarding school but looked forward every year to the pageant—the mime
Of poverty and wonder—the world of magical occurrence. As a little
Angel at the age of eight I longed to grow up and play Gabriel. The try-

Outs for the pageant made my palms sweat. How we all longed to be part
Of the mystery. To get to play Gabriel. To get to play Mary. To kneel.
To belong to A Miracle.

4

That is why
I return to cooking dinner with you, to
Flowering lettuce,
Stalks of broccoli, to cucumbers.

Ruthie

For Harout

I won't

Forget you ever, Ruthie of the imagination, of kisses and poker
And poems and music and translations of everything. Ruth—fabulous
Confessor to whom I told my secrets as you strode in your bathrobe—
Pasha of passion and patience. Ruth—friend. More then friend.
Tyrant spirit who gave us pleasure always.

In every life a friend appears who
Becomes all things—spirit, faerie tale,
Novel, poem, silly book, history book,
Map of the wilderness and the sun: Ruth,
My friend. Original. One and
Only.
I will not be lonely for her. But miss
her deeply. Wit. (It only works when it doesn't work.)
And elegant eyes.

Ruth, I wanted to give you more of my
Time. More of my love. That's what death is—
I can't give you time any more.

But you gave me: Joy. Wisdom. Sweetness.
Kind-anger. Mime. You were a dancer
In a world where people lug along. Your hands were crickets.
Your voice deep as a penny falling down a well. And now, if you
Roll your eyes in heaven—lucky angels, who will sit next to
You and love you as we do.

Waving

For Arthur Gregor

1

My bladder broke.
My child
Called.
"Stay with me," and I stayed and
Wanted to be lost,
I wanted to be lost,
To go under the leaves and
Never come back but
I stayed—losing everything—

I lived
Lost in an imaginary place.
My friends could hear me.
I knew nothing about where to find me.

2

All Women Are Prisoners

All women are like trees—
Ha ha the frond—ha ha the palm—
The lines that swirl inside the mind,
That go around the neck, the body—vine
And palm-line—
Women—I have always loved you,
I have always heard you in
My life-line, my tree line—
Let me be your diary. I want to
Speak for you—your empty seed-life,
Leaving for boarding school without a
Mother—your Canadian diplomats
Who trot down from the North
Offering a collection of syllables and
Sperm and nothing more—women I see
You sleeping in the sunlight—your
Thick lips speak but no sound comes—
And so I ask you fernwoman pinewoman
Maplewoman—let me speak for you—
I too am prisoner of lonely childlife—
Tongue and heartbreak,
Prison of the sun has touched me—I
have always been opened—let me speak
For you—I'll give you back all that you
Gave—illumination
That we seek and crave.

3

Men are prisoners also—I think
Of you—Arthur—living
In India—poet—the
First one I met when I was
Sixteen. I remember buying
A dress made out of madras
So you would think I knew about
India—I remember climbing the steps to your
House and being too shy to speak.
I remember taking your poems
In my mouth as if they were
Ripe fruit—your lines
Inside my mind—your life-line
In mine. When I spoke
No one heard me but you. So that
At sixteen I could write about
Living in a separate world
By a stream
And you—exiled from the ordinary—
Knew me—
All that I could dream. Stillness
Was then my only companion.
Arthur—you were
The prisoner—who opened your soul to me
When I wore madras—a brown dress
To look womanly.

4

Losing
Everything. Today, Arthur,
I have lost everything.
Harout—the man I love.
My black sweater. My
New brown scarf. My poem
About trees. My
Friendly disposition. Finally,
My mind.
I came home and found all
Papers strewn like white
Lungs—all my paper—
Huge white lungs
Strewn around my room. My
room of lungs. I cannot
Breathe.

5

"Rudolph Valentino has
Been back in the flesh and
Is now happily married and
Living in Paris," according
To the book by Ruth Montgomery
Called *A World Beyond*. But
Where is he? If Clark Gable
Would come back would
He please find me—flipping
Out at one-eighty
East Seventy-ninth Street,
Crying my eyes out because
Everything is getting
Lost—all old friends—
The old life—
So that I met a stranger
On the street and
Could not remember if he was once
My friend or lover—I
Cannot find my old self—
Cannot remember.

6

Here sails a woman in the middle of her life. Sets
Sail from Port of Egypt, Long Island, on the *Salty Dog*.
The *Salty Dog* is an old dumpy dinghy of a boat, a wooden
Outboard motor, vintage 1960, needing paint, needing
Varnish, not shipshape. Well, neither am I. The boat
Works. I work. The boat: not fiberglass spiffy on
The sea, but old chug-chug, resilient on the water
Of the old Long Island beerfoam green. Me. A Woman. Good-
By, Arthur, my friend.

DATE DUE